# THE AMERICAN GIRLS

**1764** KAYA, an adventurous Nez Perce girl whose deep love for horses and respect for nature nourish her spirit

**1774** FELICITY, a spunky, spritely colonial girl, full of energy and independence

**1824** JOSEFINA, a Hispanic girl whose heart and hopes are as big as the New Mexico sky

**1854** KIRSTEN, a pioneer girl of strength and spirit who settles on the frontier

**1864** ADDY, a courageous girl determined to be free in the midst of the Civil War

**1904** SAMANTHA, a bright Victorian beauty, an orphan raised by her wealthy grandmother

**1934** KIT, a clever, resourceful girl facing the Great Depression with spirit and determination

**1944** MOLLY, who schemes and dreams on the home front during World War Two

# 1775
# VERY FUNNY,
# *Elizabeth!*

BY VALERIE TRIPP

ILLUSTRATIONS DAN ANDREASEN

VIGNETTES SUSAN MCALILEY

★ American Girl™

Published by Pleasant Company Publications
Copyright © 2005 by American Girl, LLC
All rights reserved. No part of this book may be used or reproduced
in any manner whatsoever without written permission except in the
case of brief quotations embodied in critical articles and reviews.
For information, address: Book Editor, Pleasant Company Publications,
8400 Fairway Place, P.O. Box 620998, Middleton, WI 53562.

Visit our Web site at **americangirl.com**.

Printed in China
05 06 07 08 09 10 11 12 LEO 12 11 10 9 8 7 6 5 4 3 2 1

American Girl™ and its associated logos, Elizabeth™, Elizabeth Cole™, Felicity®, and
Felicity Merriman® are trademarks of American Girl, LLC.

PICTURE CREDITS
The following individuals and organizations have generously given
permission to reprint images contained in "Looking Back":
p. 67—© Historical Picture Archive/Corbis (wedding couple); pp. 68–69—*Wedding of
Stephen Beckingham and Mary Cox* (detail), William Hogarth. The Metropolitan Museum of Art,
Marquand Fund, 1936. (36.111). Photograph © 1982 The Metropolitan Museum of Art (wedding
portrait); © North Wind Picture Archives (party); Cora Ginsburg, London, 1774 (wig);
pp. 70–71—© Historical Picture Archive/Corbis (English country house); © North Wind Picture
Archives (couple); pp. 72–73—Library of Congress ("old maid" cartoon); Colonial Williamsburg
Foundation (brickmaker); Abby Aldrich Rockefeller Folk Art Center, Williamsburg, VA
(newspaper); *Sir William Pepperell and His Family*, by John Singleton Copley © North Carolina
Museum of Art/Corbis (family portrait).

Cataloging-in-Publication Data available from the Library of Congress.

TO SALLY WOOD,
WITH LOVE AND THANKS
FOR HER INFORMATION AND INSPIRATION

# TABLE OF CONTENTS

ELIZABETH'S FAMILY
AND FRIENDS

## ELIZABETH
*A mischievous,
independent-minded girl
growing up in the
colonies in 1775*

## FELICITY
*Elizabeth's best friend,
her good companion in
lessons and fun*

## ANNABELLE
*Elizabeth's snobby older
sister, who thinks only
of finding a husband*

## MISS MANDERLY
*Elizabeth and Felicity's
teacher, a gracious
gentlewoman*

LORD
HARRY LACEY
*An English nobleman
in need of a wife*

MISS
PRISCILLA LACEY
*Lord Harry's older sister—
a very difficult woman*

# CHAPTER ONE

## THE MERRIEST GIRLS IN VIRGINIA

Elizabeth Cole quickened her steps so that she was even farther ahead of her sister Annabelle. It was a very cold, very clear December day. Elizabeth, in her sky-blue cloak, looked like a brisk, busy bluebird as she hurried along the main street of Williamsburg. She just *had* to get to Mr. Merriman's store before Annabelle did. Elizabeth glanced over her shoulder and saw that she need not worry. Annabelle was walking at a ladylike pace and lagging far behind.

*Good!* thought Elizabeth. Quick as a wink, she dashed up the steps to Mr. Merriman's store. She opened the door and poked her head inside. Her very best friend, Felicity Merriman, was waiting so close to the door that the girls practically bumped noses, which made them burst into giggles.

Mr. Merriman smiled at Elizabeth and Felicity. "You two are the merriest girls in Virginia," he said. He bowed to Elizabeth and asked, "How are you today, Miss Elizabeth?"

Elizabeth bobbed a curtsy, even though the part of her that was curtsying was still outside the door. "I'm very well, thank you, Mr. Merriman," she said politely. Mr. Merriman turned back to his work and Elizabeth whispered to Felicity, "Annabelle is coming. Is this a good day to play our joke?"

"Aye," said Felicity. She tilted her head toward the back corner of the store where her father's apprentice, Ben, was up on a ladder, stocking shelves.

Elizabeth glanced at Ben, and then she and Felicity shared a delighted grin. In some ways, Elizabeth and Felicity were different. Elizabeth was rather small for her age; Felicity was tall. Elizabeth had golden hair and a sunny, even temperament. She was good at thinking and planning, while Felicity rushed headlong into things and had a gingery temper to match her gingery red

2

hair. Elizabeth came from a family of Loyalists who believed that it was best for the king of England to rule the colonies. Felicity and her family thought some of the king's laws were unfair, so they were Patriots. But in all

*King George and Queen Charlotte*

the ways that were really important, Elizabeth and Felicity were alike. They both loved to read. They both loved to be out-of-doors. They both loved animals. They both loved to laugh. And most of all, they both loved being best friends.

Elizabeth ducked back outside the door and saw that Annabelle had stopped at the edge of a slushy puddle made of yesterday's melted snow. Elizabeth watched her sister shudder with horror, lift her petticoat, and mince her way around the puddle as if it were a nest of snakes. Elizabeth waited patiently. She was used to waiting for Annabelle. Even though Elizabeth was younger and smaller, she was much quicker than Annabelle.

Just as Elizabeth expected, when Annabelle drew near she scolded, "'Tis unladylike to walk so fast, Bitsy."

"You are quite right," Elizabeth answered

sweetly, though she did not like being called "Bitsy" any more than she liked being scolded. "I should have walked slowly, as you did." Elizabeth dabbed at her eyes with her handkerchief. "I'm sure I look a sight! Hurrying in this cold weather has made my eyes red and runny, while *your* eyes look bright and clear."

Annabelle smiled and preened. She was a very pretty young lady and especially proud of her big, beautiful brown eyes.

"Just the other day, a young man told me that the first things he noticed were bright, clear eyes and good, sound teeth," said Elizabeth. She went on, as if she were thinking aloud. "Now who told me that? Oh, yes. 'Twas Ben."

"Ben?" repeated Annabelle, suddenly very alert and interested. She adjusted her hat, smoothed her cloak, and marched past Elizabeth into Mr. Merriman's store. Elizabeth swallowed a laugh as she followed. She and Felicity knew very well that Annabelle was smitten with Ben and always eager for attention from him. The joke Elizabeth and Felicity had planned for today depended upon the fact that Annabelle was sweet on Ben.

4

Annabelle spotted Ben and aimed straight for him like an arrow shot from a bow.

"Good day, Miss Cole," said Mr. Merriman to Annabelle as she flew by. "May I help you?"

Annabelle stopped and looked at Mr. Merriman with consternation. *He* was not the one she was interested in! Elizabeth and Felicity were worried, too; their joke would not work if Mr. Merriman helped Annabelle.

"Ah, oh, no thank you, Mr. Merriman!" said Annabelle hastily. "I beg you will not trouble yourself, sir. Ben can help me."

"Very well," said Mr. Merriman. He went to the storeroom. Elizabeth and Felicity sighed small sighs of relief. They pretended to be looking at whistles, but out of the corners of their eyes, they watched Annabelle.

"Ben!" said Annabelle loudly. She startled poor Ben so much that he lurched, wobbled, and almost fell off the ladder. Ben turned, and Annabelle smiled flirtatiously up at him. "I'm here for ribbon," she said. "Do help me."

Ben climbed down the ladder and took his place behind the counter. Annabelle leaned toward him and opened her eyes very wide. She asked, "What color ribbon will look best with my eyes, do you think?"

"Brown," said Ben.

"Oh, la!" twittered Annabelle, as if Ben had said something clever. "But brown is not very festive. And the ribbon's to trim my very best dress—the dress I'll be wearing if I am invited to any Christmas parties, concerts, dinners, balls . . ." Annabelle fluttered her eyelashes and smiled a smile that showed all her teeth as she said significantly, "or weddings."

Ben squinted at Annabelle's toothy smile and flirty, fluttery eyes. "Miss Cole," he said, "are you quite well? Is there something in your eye? Do you have a toothache?"

"Oh, la!" Annabelle said again, smiling even more toothily and fluttering her eyelashes even faster. "I know you admire bright eyes and sound teeth. A little bird told me that they are the first things you notice."

Elizabeth poked Felicity. Their joke was working!

Ben looked puzzled. "Bright eyes and sound teeth?" he repeated. He thought for a moment and then said, "Well, yes, they are, Miss Cole—when I'm looking at a horse."

"A *horse?*" squawked Annabelle.

Ben nodded.

Elizabeth and Felicity covered their mouths to smother their laughter, but one or two giggles sneaked out.

Annabelle whirled around to face them, her smile now sunk to a sour frown, her eyes now narrow and angry. "You!" she snarled at Elizabeth. "You tricked me!" And with that, Annabelle stamped her foot and stormed out of the store without another word.

Befuddled Ben shrugged and climbed back up the ladder.

"Elizabeth," Felicity said, "Annabelle is annoyed."

"No doubt," said Elizabeth cheerfully. "But it was well worth it!" Elizabeth smiled widely and fluttered her eyelashes in imitation of Annabelle. *"Nnnn-eighhhh,"* she neighed softly, like a very quiet horse.

Felicity laughed and shook

her head. "I remember when you used to be afraid of Annabelle," she said.

"'Twas you who taught me to stand up to Annabelle Bananabelle!" Elizabeth replied. "Mind, she still snips at me as much as ever. But I don't let her scolding bother me anymore. 'Tis just part of her silliness. And now I know that it is more fun to laugh than to be afraid."

"You and I laugh," said Felicity, "but doesn't Annabelle get angry at you when you tease her?"

"Well, yes," said Elizabeth, "though of course I tease her only because she is my sister and I love her and I want to help her."

"To help her?" Felicity asked.

"Indeed, yes," said Elizabeth. "I tease Annabelle to show her how ridiculous she's acting. I know that underneath all of Annabelle's airs and sillinesses, she has a sense of humor and a sensible brain. I tease her to poke and prod her into being her true self. She will thank me someday."

"I don't think she is going to thank you today," Felicity said. "In fact, I think you had better hurry along after her now and try to calm her down before she gets home."

"You are quite right," said Elizabeth. "I will see you tomorrow at lessons!"

The two friends bobbed happy curtsies, and then Elizabeth left.

As she skipped down the steps outside the store, Elizabeth saw that Annabelle's annoyance seemed to have made her forget all about walking at a ladylike pace. Elizabeth had to trot to catch up to her sister.

When she did, Annabelle snapped, "Very funny, Elizabeth! You made me act like a ninny in front of Ben. Bright eyes and sound teeth, hah! You knew perfectly well he was talking about horses! How *could* you?"

"'Twas only a joke," said Elizabeth. "We meant it all in fun."

"A joke?" sputtered Annabelle. "Now Ben thinks I am a nincompoop."

Elizabeth privately believed that Ben had *always* thought Annabelle was a nincompoop—when he thought of her at all. But Elizabeth said soothingly, "Now, Annabelle, 'twas only *Ben*."

"Ben comes from a very fine family in Yorktown," said Annabelle. "I consider him an eligible beau. He fancies himself a Patriot and says he's going to join the army when he finishes his apprenticeship, but I am sure that I could talk him out of *that* wrongheaded notion. In any case, I'm quite put out that now, thanks to you, he may never come courting."

"Courting?" said Elizabeth. Now it was her turn to sputter! Annabelle was always flirting, but Elizabeth thought flirtatiousness, like scolding, was just another part of her sister's silliness. "You can't be serious, Annabelle! It's not as if you are truly thinking of becoming engaged or getting married. You are but sixteen years of age!"

Annabelle stopped and faced Elizabeth. "Sixteen is not too young to begin courting, or even to marry. Indeed, if I wait too long, all the best gentlemen will be snapped up by other young ladies," she said with a greedy glint in her eyes. "My whole future happiness depends upon marrying well. I must be mistress of my own house. Finding a husband and making a good marriage is a serious business, the sooner begun, the better."

"I'm glad I am only ten years old, and marriage and men are no worry of mine yet," Elizabeth said. "I would hate to change my life so greatly, and to

leave Mama and Father. I love our home and our life just the way they are here in Williamsburg. I want my life to stay the same forever."

"Hmph!" snorted Annabelle crossly. "With your help and that of your fine friend Felicity, *my* life will stay the same forever, too. I'll be stuck at home and die an old maid." The more she ranted, the more Annabelle worked herself up into a lather. "I won't stand for any more of your teasing!" she said hotly. "I am going to put a stop to it. I shall speak to Mama and tell her how you tricked me today. Come, Bitsy!"

As she followed Annabelle home, Elizabeth was not very worried. Annabelle loved to tattle, and told tales on Elizabeth nearly every day. In fact, Annabelle's complaints came so fast and frequently that Elizabeth had noticed her parents hardly listened to them anymore. So Elizabeth calmly went with Annabelle into the parlor where her mother and father were talking, and she calmly waited for Annabelle to begin pouring out her disgruntlements.

But Annabelle did not have a chance to say a word. As soon as he saw the two girls making their curtsies, Mr. Cole said, "There you are! Come in.

11

Make haste. Be seated. I should like to speak to you, Annabelle."

Her father spoke so very seriously that it sounded to Elizabeth as if *Annabelle* was the one in trouble this time. Elizabeth, full of curiosity, sat on a stiff side chair and picked up her stitchery. She kept her eyes cast down upon it, waiting eagerly to hear what her father had to say. Even Annabelle was quiet for a change.

Mr. Cole seemed to be unsure how to begin. "Ah, *ahem*," he said, clearing his throat.

*What ails Father?* thought Elizabeth. *This dilly-dallying is unlike him.*

"Annabelle, my dear," said Mr. Cole at last. "I have here a letter from the Honorable Miss Priscilla Lacey. Her father, Lord Hugh Lacey, was a friend of mine in England. I conducted some business for him, as you may recall."

Annabelle blurted out, "Well, no, Father, I—"

But Mr. Cole held up his hand to stop her. Now that he had begun to speak, he did not want to be interrupted. "Lord Hugh Lacey died a few years ago," he said. "His son, Harry, inherited his title and became Lord Harry. Miss Lacey has been running the estate and the household for Harry, who is much younger than she is. But Harry is now of an age to marry. And so Miss Lacey has written to me to suggest . . . that is, she asks . . ." Mr. Cole cleared his throat again, then came out with it all in a rush. "Miss Lacey proposes that her brother should marry *you*."

Elizabeth was so surprised that she pricked herself with her needle.

"Me?" Annabelle leaped to her feet and squeaked, "Yes! I will, Father! I will marry Lord Hugh and move to England, and gladly!"

"Lord Harry," Mr. Cole corrected.

"What? Oh! Oh, yes, yes, of course," flubbered Annabelle, bouncing. "Lord Larry. No, Lord *Harry!* Yes, I meant I'll marry Lord *Harry*, of course!"

"Annabelle, my child," said Mrs. Cole. "Do stop and think, I beg you! Marrying is the most serious decision a young woman makes. Remember that once you are married, you are married forever."

"Yes," Elizabeth piped up. "And England is very, very far away! And also you don't know Lord Harry. Perhaps you will not like him."

"Pishposh!" said Annabelle. "He is a lord. I will

be a lady. That is all I need to know."

"Don't be hasty!" said Mrs. Cole. "Marrying will mean the end of the youthful freedom you now enjoy, when you have only your father and me to please and yourself to amuse. A married woman, especially a lady married to such a man as Lord Harry, has many responsibilities. 'Twill not all be riding in fine carriages, wearing fancy gowns, and going to parties and balls. There will be a huge country house to be mistress of, with many servants to manage, and most likely another large house in London."

"London!" Annabelle exclaimed ecstatically. She clasped her hands together and rose up on her toes in delight. Elizabeth could tell that her mother's sensible warnings, which were meant to bring Annabelle down to earth, were having quite the opposite effect. Annabelle wasn't thinking about how far away England was or the many responsibilities her new life would bring. She was thinking only about the romance and prestige. Annabelle gushed, "Oh, I want to marry Lord Harry as soon as possible!"

Mr. Cole looked at Mrs. Cole, who nodded slowly. Then Mr. Cole said, "Very well! I will send a positive answer to Miss Priscilla. She and Lord Harry are visiting relatives in New York just now. I will write and invite them to come here to Williamsburg straightaway. We will work out the marriage contract and the details of  the wedding then. We will announce the engagement at Christmastide, and the wedding can take place in February."

"On Saint Valentine's Day!" swooned Annabelle. "Oh, it will be so romantic!"

"As you wish," said Mr. Cole. "Then you'll sail to England in the spring. Well! I'll go now and begin my letter to Miss Priscilla."

He bowed. Elizabeth, Annabelle, and Mrs. Cole curtsied as he left.

Immediately Annabelle turned to her mother. "Oh, Mama," she crowed, "isn't it wonderful? I'm to be married. Aren't you pleased?"

Mrs. Cole patted Annabelle's hand. "I am pleased to see you so happy, my dear," she said, "and to know that you'll be safe in England. But I worry—"

"Gracious!" Annabelle interrupted. "You mustn't waste time worrying, Mama! There's so much to do! We must prepare for Lord Harry and Miss Priscilla. And I shall need a wedding dress! And clothes for my new life as Lady Lacey!" Annabelle was floating with joy and gloating with satisfaction. "Just think! Every young lady in Williamsburg will envy me when she hears the news! Oh, Mama, we must have a big party at Christmastide to announce the engagement. And I will be the center of attention. Our party must be one that no one will ever forget."

Elizabeth smiled down at her stitchery. She could not quite believe that Annabelle—Annabelle Bananabelle!—was *truly* going to be engaged. But visitors from England and a party with Annabelle as the belle of the ball? That *truly* sounded like a Christmas season full of opportunity for mischief-making and fun for Elizabeth and Felicity, the merriest girls in Virginia.

# CHAPTER TWO

## TARTS FOR TEA

*Tap, tap, tap!* Elizabeth's toes tapped Felicity's underneath the table.

*Thump.* Felicity's foot softly thumped Elizabeth's foot in response.

The foot signals were a method that Elizabeth and Felicity had invented to communicate secretly during lessons. They used the foot signals partly out of respect for their teacher, Miss Manderly. They liked her very much, and never wanted her to think that they weren't paying attention while she was teaching them. But mostly they used the foot signals to get around Annabelle, who always poked her nosy little nose into their private conversations and noticed when they exchanged meaningful glances.

Elizabeth's three gentle taps meant, "Let's tease Annabelle."

Felicity's gentle thump meant, "Yes!"

The two friends had strict rules about teasing Annabelle: No lies. Nothing unkind or mean-spirited. Nothing that hurt, like a pinch or an insult. And only for a good reason. Today, for example, they were going to tease Annabelle to help her stop sounding so snobbish!

"Only the very *finest* lace on my night shifts, of course," said Annabelle, droning on and on to Miss Manderly. "Nothing less will do for the wife of Lord Harry."

Elizabeth thought that if she heard the name "Lord Harry" one more time, steam would come out of her ears like the steam coming out of the spout of the tea kettle! All morning Annabelle had rattled on about marrying Lord Harry, the grand party to be held to announce that she was going to marry Lord Harry, all the frippery and finery she would shortly need because she was going to marry Lord Harry, and how important and grand a lady she would be after she did marry Lord Harry. Now, even though fragrant mint tea had been poured, Annabelle was

turned away from the table,
showing Miss Manderly a piece
of the snowy white linen that
her wedding night shifts and other
new clothes were to be made of, for
goodness sake! On and on and on Annabelle talked.

*Let the teasing begin,* thought Elizabeth.

Elizabeth saw Felicity slip a tart onto Annabelle's
plate, then another tart, then another, then another,
then another, one tart on top of the other. Felicity hid
another tart in the folds of Annabelle's napkin.

Elizabeth moved Annabelle's teacup and saucer
so that they were just behind Annabelle's elbow.
Then she filled the cup to the brim.

Finally, Miss Manderly said, "Annabelle, my
dear, let us turn and drink our tea now, before it
grows cold."

As Annabelle turned to take her tea, her elbow
knocked over her filled-to-the-brim cup and then
toppled the teetery tower of tarts on her plate so that
they tumbled onto the tea table. "Oh, dear me!" said
Annabelle. When she picked up her napkin to mop
up the tea, a tart fell out and plopped into her lap.
"Oh, dear me!" said Annabelle again, lifting the tart

from her lap with her fingertips. "Look at this mess!"

Elizabeth and Felicity hid their smiles inside their teacups and innocently drank their tea.

Elizabeth thought she detected a twinkle in Miss Manderly's eye when the teacher chided Annabelle gently, saying, "It is not good manners to put quite so many tarts onto one's plate, Annabelle."

"But I didn't," protested Annabelle. "'Twas those two!" She glared at Elizabeth and Felicity and opened her mouth as if she was about to speak angrily at them. But then she put her nose in the air and said in a very superior voice, "The wife of Lord Harry must be well-mannered at all times."

"Yes, indeed," said Miss Manderly. She stood. "I will go ask the maid to fetch more tarts."

The minute Miss Manderly left, Annabelle gave Elizabeth and Felicity a condescending look. "You two are just jealous," she said.

"Not at all!" Elizabeth said. "We think it's suspicious that Miss Lacey has had to come all the way to Virginia to find a wife for her brother. There must be a reason why no young lady in England will marry Lord Harry."

"That's right," said Felicity. "We'd never marry

any silly lord we'd never met! He may be just terrible. He may be dull and boring, or gloomy!"

"Yes," joked Elizabeth, "Lord Harry may not be very merry. And who knows what he looks like? Lord Harry may look scary or be very, very hairy!"

Felicity and Elizabeth snickered.

Annabelle ignored the joke. "I am sure Lord Harry is a perfect gentleman," she said. "After all, he is a lord, which means he is a nobleman."

"Being a nobleman doesn't mean he is a noble person," said Elizabeth. "Having a title like 'Lord' or 'Lady' may be important in England, but I have noticed that here in the colonies, people think for themselves and they respect people for what they *do*. Here people are considered noble if they *act* nobly."

Annabelle flickered her fingers as if Elizabeth's idea were no more than a pesky fly. "You're just parroting Felicity, your Patriot friend," she sniffed.

"Perhaps," said Elizabeth. "But I like the way it is here, where people are independent and can work hard and make their lives better. People prove their worthiness. The respect they earn has nothing to do with their names."

"I pray you will not spout such nonsense about

21

independence and lack of respect for nobility in front of Lord Harry and Miss Priscilla," said Annabelle. "They'd be shocked to see that we have a little Patriot in our family. Besides, Bitsy, you're just too young to understand. You will feel differently when you are older. Indeed, both of you two uncivilized brats will feel differently as soon as I am married, and you see the respect my new position brings me."

"No," Elizabeth began heatedly, "we—"

"Young ladies," said Miss Manderly from the doorway. "That will do."

All three girls sat up straight and silent.

"Annabelle," said Miss Manderly, "I think you know better than to refer to your sister and her friend as 'uncivilized brats.'"

Annabelle flushed. "But—" she began.

Miss Manderly came to the table and put her hand on top of Annabelle's to stop her from talking. It soon became apparent that Miss Manderly had overheard a great deal of the girls' argument. She turned to Felicity and Elizabeth and said, "Annabelle is quite right. Her intended, Lord Lacey, is a nobleman, and as such, he is a very desirable husband. Annabelle is fortunate to have had an offer of marriage from him. If he is a good and decent man, every young lady must envy her that good fortune. Do you understand, young ladies?"

"Yes, ma'am," said Elizabeth and Felicity together.

Then Miss Manderly spoke to Annabelle in a serious voice. "Marriage is a choice, Annabelle," Miss Manderly said. "It is not the only road to happiness for a woman, or the easiest road, either. Especially here in the colonies, it is possible for a woman to stand on her own two feet and make an independent life for herself that is full and satisfying, as I have. As a nobleman's wife you will not have that independence. There will be many strict rules of behavior and etiquette you will be expected to follow. You will have many duties and responsibilities."

Annabelle began to look solemn, but she perked up when Miss Manderly said, "However, you will be entitled to the privilege, respect, and admiration accorded those ladies in the very highest ranks of society if you handle your position as the wife of Lord Harry well."

Annabelle tossed her head, squared her

shoulders, and smirked. She looked pleased at the way Miss Manderly made it sound as if she had won a great and rare prize in Lord Harry.

Neither Felicity nor Elizabeth said a word. But under the table, their feet banged into one another. *Clonk!* That was the secret foot signal that meant, "Annabelle Bananabelle is so annoying!"

All afternoon on the day that Lord Harry and Miss Priscilla were expected, Elizabeth teased Annabelle. Every time a carriage passed by outside the bedchamber where the sisters were waiting, Elizabeth would fly to the window and gasp, "Is that the Laceys' carriage?"

Annabelle would leap from her seat as if a spring had sprung beneath her, yank out the rags that were curling her side curls, and fly downstairs to the entrance hall in order to be in place when the front door opened.

Of course, the carriage never was the Laceys'. After five false alarms, five mad rushes down the stairs, five out-of-breath trudges back up, and five re-tyings of the curling rags, Annabelle was hot and cross. She plunked herself down in her chair and announced, "You will not fool me again, Bitsy."

Elizabeth sat quietly for a minute or two. Then she cocked her ear toward the window yet again. "I hear a carriage," she said. She went to the window. "I think it is really the Laceys this time! A small lady and a tall man are coming to our front door. Come look, Annabelle."

"No!" said Annabelle. "This is just more of your nonsense, Elizabeth. Say what you like. I am not going to move."

Suddenly the chamber door burst open and Mrs. Cole appeared. "Annabelle!" she said. "Come downstairs immediately! The Laceys have arrived. Make haste, dear child! You, too, Elizabeth, my love."

Annabelle shot up out of her chair with a howl and stumbled over her own feet in her hurry to follow her mother out the door and down the stairs to the entrance hall. She yanked the curling rags from her hair as she ran. Elizabeth was close behind Annabelle. She did not want to miss a moment!

Mr. Cole was waiting in the hall with their

*Mr. Cole made polite introductions.*

guests. Elizabeth saw that Miss Priscilla Lacey was tiny and wore her hair in very tightly wound curls that quivered constantly, as if they were indignant. She had a very sharp, pointed nose and very sharp brown eyes. Lord Harry Lacey, by contrast, was a young giant. He had long arms, big hands, and a big, beaky nose. His eyebrows were as thick as caterpillars and they were raised up, which made him look surprised and a bit confused as to where he was and why he was there.

Mr. Cole made polite introductions. "Lord Harry, Miss Lacey," he said, "permit me to introduce my wife, Mrs. Cole, and my daughters, Annabelle and Elizabeth."

"Welcome!" said Mrs. Cole graciously. All the ladies curtsied and Mr. Cole bowed. Annabelle's curtsy was a bit wobbly because she was smiling up at Lord Harry, who blushed. Miss Priscilla waggled her head at him to remind him to bow.

"Oh! Right-oh, Prissy!" Lord Harry said as he bent in a bungled bow.

"Well!" said Mrs. Cole brightly. "Shall we go to the parlor for tea?" She turned to lead the way.

Lord Harry boomed, "Right-oh!" with so

much enthusiasm that Miss Priscilla winced. He galumphed into the parlor eagerly.

Poor Lord Harry! Elizabeth felt sorry for him as tea was served. His teacup looked like a thimble in his giant hand, and he was too big for his chair. He looked like a horse who'd been asked into the parlor. He had just popped a whole biscuit into his mouth when Mr. Cole made matters worse by turning everyone's attention to him.

"Lord Harry," said Mr. Cole, "here in Virginia, the conflict between Loyalists and Patriots is becoming more serious and dangerous every day. The Royal Governor and his family have had to abandon their palace and leave Williamsburg. You have just come from New York. What do you think of the situation there?"

At the word "think," Lord Harry's eyebrows shot up in alarm and he looked nervously at his sister. Elizabeth could see that Lord Harry was uncomfortable being asked what he thought. She guessed that he was used to being *told* by his sister what he thought. And indeed, while Lord Harry was still munching, Miss Priscilla spoke for him.

"Dreadful," said Miss Priscilla crisply.

"Right-oh, Prissy," mumbled Lord Harry around the biscuit in his mouth.

"Have another biscuit," Mrs. Cole said to him kindly. Then she and Mr. Cole took pity on Lord Harry and began a lively conversation that did not require any participation from him.

Miss Priscilla turned to Annabelle, who was seated next to her, and took hold of both her hands. "You are an enchanting child, Arabelle!" Miss Priscilla said. "Harry is fortunate indeed."

Annabelle sneaked a peek at Lord Harry and glowed. She was too pleased to correct Miss Priscilla's mispronunciation of her name.

"I'll take you under my wing," Miss Priscilla went on to Annabelle. "After all, you are my future sister-in-law! I'll teach you how ladies and gentlemen behave in the very highest level of society so that you won't be embarrassed when we're back in England."

"How kind of you!" gushed Annabelle, who did not understand that she had just been insulted. "Manners here in the colonies are shocking." She tilted her head toward Elizabeth and sighed, "Mama and I try to set a good example, and Bitsy and I *do* take lessons with a gentlewoman, but Bitsy has picked up some horridly rough manners from her colonial friend, Felicity."

"You poor dear Suzabelle!" said Miss Priscilla. "How terrible for you to be ashamed of your little sister's manners."

"Indeed yes!" said Annabelle. She shot a self-satisfied smile over her shoulder at Elizabeth.

Elizabeth batted her eyelashes and smiled a pretend smile back. *Suzabelle, indeed!* Elizabeth suspected that Miss Priscilla knew perfectly well that Annabelle's name was *Anna*belle. It seemed almost as if Miss Priscilla had deliberately used the wrong name to show that she was so superior, she did not *need* to remember what sort of "belle" the elder Miss Cole was.

Now Miss Priscilla spoke up to get Mrs. Cole's attention. "My dear Mrs. Cole," Miss Priscilla said. "It's all decided. I am going to make a pet of your darling elder daughter. I shall give her guidance and advice to prepare her for her life in England." Then Miss Priscilla turned her pinpoint eyes on Elizabeth. "Shall I teach you, too, Little One?" she asked.

Everyone waited for Elizabeth to answer. At first Elizabeth wanted to say, "No, thank you! *I'm* not the one who's going to marry poor harried Lord Harry and move to England, thank goodness! Besides, my manners are just fine." But then Elizabeth had a thought. How could she say no to such a wonderful opportunity to annoy Annabelle, who surely did not want to share Miss Priscilla's attention with her? And so Elizabeth answered Miss Priscilla with enthusiasm. "Oh, yes, please," she said. "Do teach me along with Annabelle."

Miss Priscilla beamed. "You see, Mrs. Cole, how enthusiastic Little One is?" she said. "It is the wish of her heart to be instructed by me, along with her sister. May I have your permission to do so?"

"Yes, indeed," said Mrs. Cole. "Thank you!"

"Yes, thank you, Miss Priscilla!" said Elizabeth. She was pleased to see Annabelle's smile slide down to a frown. Elizabeth held a plate out to Annabelle and said impishly, "Look, Annabelle, tarts for tea! Your favorites! Mind you don't take too many."

# CHAPTER THREE

## MISS PRISS

The very next morning, Miss Priscilla began instructing Annabelle and Elizabeth in the ways aristocratic ladies behaved in England. When the sisters came to breakfast, Miss Priscilla sang out, "Dorabelle and Little One! You are wearing such sweet dresses. I had one in that style long ago, when it was fashionable. It makes me feel quite young to see that style again. But of course, in England, a lady in the highest circle of society must always look fashionable and up-to-date, not dowdy as a milkmaid."

Annabelle nodded, wide-eyed. She accepted

Miss Priscilla's instructive comment as if it were a precious jewel of wisdom. But Elizabeth saw that the comment was nothing more than a criticism disguised as a compliment.

When the girls sat at the table, Miss Priscilla smiled and said, "I am amused by your hair, Clarabelle. And yours, too, Little One. You look like dear little curly-haired lambs. Of course, ladies in England would never be seen with even *one* hair out of place."

Annabelle had taken extra trouble that morning to fix her hair in an elaborate manner in order to impress Miss Priscilla. But now she sheepishly pulled her cap down to cover her curls, and nudged Elizabeth to do the same. Elizabeth ignored her and served herself some breakfast ham.

As the girls ate, Miss Priscilla laughed a tinkling, mirthless laugh. She said, "Isabelle and Little One, I do admire your healthy appetites. You eat a tremendous amount! Of course, ladies in England are delicate and consider it impolite to eat so heartily."

Annabelle's cheeks pinked to the color of the ham on her plate and she put her fork down quickly. Elizabeth continued chewing. She was beginning to regret having agreed to be included in Miss Priscilla's aristocratic lady lessons—and their very first breakfast together was not even over!

As the days went on, Elizabeth more and more regretted being included. She grew tired of being told, day after day, how things were done in England. She grew tired of being with Miss Priscilla from morning till night, too. They hardly ever saw Lord Harry. Whenever he blundered into a room where Miss Priscilla was seated with Annabelle and Elizabeth, he'd stop short. He'd blush shyly at Annabelle, take one look at his sister's impatient eyes and irritated curls, then skitter away as quickly as possible. Elizabeth understood why. Miss Priscilla's sharp, pointed eyes found faults in him, too, which she pointed out with sharp, pointed comments. So Lord Harry spent most of his days following Mr. Cole around like a faithful dog or meandering around Williamsburg. One day, Elizabeth saw him standing with Ben looking at the horses in the neighbors' paddock. Except at tea and dinner, where he never said a word because his sister always spoke for him, Elizabeth and Annabelle saw Lord Harry very rarely.

At last an afternoon came when
Elizabeth could slip away. Annabelle
and Miss Priscilla were going to
the milliner's shop to choose a new
stomacher for Annabelle's best dress.
Annabelle, who was very particular

about her appearance, stood at the mirror by the
front door and adjusted the bow on her hat over and
over again. Just when she was finally satisfied, Miss
Priscilla looked at the bow, shivered with distaste,
and re-tied it for her.

"You mustn't look like a country mouse when
you are out in public, Minabelle," she said, "even in
such an insignificant town as this. I pray you will try
to look your best on the evening of the engagement
party. Your mother and I have invited people from
only the very highest circle of society, and it would
not do to be embarrassed in front of them." She
sighed and added haughtily, "Of course, thanks
to those dreadful, hot-headed Patriots, there are
not many Loyalists left here in Williamsburg." She
frowned, tilted Annabelle's hat, then said, "Come
along now."

As soon as Miss Priscilla and Annabelle were

out the door, Elizabeth rushed to Felicity's house and told her woes to her friend.

"Miss Priscilla's idea of instructing Annabelle and me is to tell us everything that we do wrong, which seems to be everything that we do," Elizabeth said to Felicity. "According to her, Annabelle and I don't dress, stand, walk, talk, sit, eat, drink, or *breathe* the way aristocratic ladies do in England! All I can say is that those ladies in England must be miserable! They have so many rules to follow. I am very glad that *I* am not moving to England!"

"I am glad, too," said Felicity, smiling at her friend. "Does Annabelle *really* want to marry Lord Harry?"

"It seems so," said Elizabeth, "though she still does not really know him at all. They are never allowed to be alone together. If Lord Harry ever does happen to run into Annabelle and me, Annabelle smiles at him, he blushes shyly at her, and then he scurries off. When the whole family is gathered for tea and dinner, he only ever says one thing." Elizabeth pretended to be Lord Harry and said in a deep voice, "Right-oh!"

The girls giggled.

"At least he sounds agreeable," said Felicity. "Do you think he's nice?"

"Yes, I do," Elizabeth said, "and I think you would, too, Felicity. He *is* rather a tongue-tied, clumsy bumbler when his sister is around, but that's just because she makes him so very nervous. He seems to be happiest out-of-doors, and he's very at ease with dogs and horses. He's sort of like a horse himself."

"Then I would certainly like him!" said Felicity, who adored horses.

"I do like Lord Harry," said Elizabeth, "but I'd think more highly of him if he didn't let his sister bully him as he does." She sighed. "Miss Priscilla is so very tiresome. I dread the time I spend with her. And Annabelle makes it worse. First she puts on hoity-toity airs trying to impress Miss Priscilla. Then, when Miss Priscilla criticizes her, Annabelle just accepts it. I wish I knew a way to shake Annabelle awake and poke and prod her into seeing how ridiculous she's acting and how silly she is to let Miss Priss bully *her,* too."

Felicity smiled slyly. "Oh," she said lightly, "I think you *do* know a way to poke and prod Annabelle."

Elizabeth grinned gleefully, because underneath the table, Felicity's toes were tapping hers. *Tap, tap, tap!*

❧

Elizabeth did her best. Conscientiously, every morning at breakfast for the next three days, Elizabeth teased Annabelle with tried-and-true tricks that she and Felicity had invented. To torment Annabelle even more, Elizabeth acted like a prim, proper, perfect little "Miss Priss" herself.

The first day, Elizabeth put salt in Annabelle's tea instead of sugar, which made Annabelle turn very red in the face and rush from the room coughing and sputtering.

"Gracious, Sarabelle!" Miss Priscilla called out after Annabelle. "Ladies in England never gulp their tea! And they never run out of the room without making a proper curtsy!"

"*Tsk, tsk, tsk,*" Elizabeth tsked. She sipped *her* tea slowly and carefully.

On the second day, Elizabeth secretly slipped a little bit of an icicle down the back of Annabelle's dress, which made Annabelle whoop, leap up from her chair, and run from the room squealing.

"Gracious, Corabelle!" Miss Priscilla called out after her. "Ladies in England never whoop! And as I told you before, they never run out of the room without making a proper curtsy!"

Elizabeth shook her head sadly and silently. She sat straight and still in *her* chair.

On the third day, Elizabeth hid a live spider in among Annabelle's slices of toast, which made Annabelle shriek in terror and push her plate away with such force that it knocked over a bowl of prunes in gooey juice and spilled the prunes and juice all over the table. Then Annabelle ran from the room howling.

"Gracious, Florabelle!" Miss Priscilla called out after her. "Ladies in England never knock things over! And must I tell you *again* that a lady never runs out of the room without making a proper curtsy?"

Elizabeth sighed quietly and lifted *her* toast with dainty fingers.

The fourth day was the day of the party to announce Annabelle's engagement to Lord Harry. Elizabeth had planned to try the teetery tower of tarts trick again, but she decided not to at the last minute because her mother and father had joined them at breakfast, which was most unusual and, as it turned out, dreadful for Elizabeth.

"I am here to give you good news, Elizabeth," said Mr. Cole. "Miss Priscilla has most generously offered to take you along when she and Lord Harry and Annabelle sail for England. Your mother and I have agreed. Miss Priscilla herself will announce this additional good news at the engagement party tonight."

Elizabeth gasped. She was stunned speechless. Her heart beat fast, her face flushed red, and her jaw fell open. She was going to England, too? It was the most horrifying idea she had ever heard!

"I can see that you are as amazed at the great generosity of Miss Priscilla's invitation as we were," Mr. Cole went on. "You understand that the move to England will be very advantageous for you. You will be lifted into a higher level of society than we enjoy here in Virginia, which means that you will have better prospects for marriage eventually and, meanwhile, better education and training to be a lady."

In desperation, Elizabeth turned to her mother, but before she could say a word, Mrs. Cole said gently, "Your father and I have been trying to find

a way to remove both you and Annabelle from the dangerous political situation here in the colonies, Elizabeth, my love. The future grows more uncertain for us Loyalists in Virginia every day."

"Yes, indeed!" Miss Priscilla cut in. "We must take you away from these wild, uncivilized Patriot hot-heads!"

Mrs. Cole smiled sadly at Elizabeth. "We will be brokenhearted to part with you, dear Elizabeth," she said, "but we are thinking of your future and of your safety. And it will comfort us to know that you and Annabelle are together."

Good manners prevented Elizabeth from shouting out, "No! I won't go!" She swallowed hard, then said in a shaky voice, "Mama, Father, with all respect, I beg you to believe me when I say that I do not want to go."

Annabelle added, "And I don't want her to, either! She's a minx and a mischief-maker!" But no one paid any attention to Annabelle.

"Ha, ha, ha," Miss Priscilla laughed gratingly. "We all know that you *do* want to come to England, Little One. Did you not beg to be included in my instructions about how to behave in England? And for the past three days at breakfast, your manners have been impeccable. You will fit into aristocratic society perfectly. *You* have not gulped your tea, whooped, or spilled the prunes. You have never run out of the room without making a proper curtsy, which, as you know, your sister has done over and over again, despite my constant reminders!"

"But *I* made Annabelle do all those things!" said Elizabeth. "I played tricks on her."

Annabelle whirled to face Miss Priscilla. "That is what I have been trying to tell you!" she said with exasperation.

But Miss Priscilla just laughed again. "It is kind of you to try to excuse your sister's mistakes, Little One," she said. "But you need not. And don't worry. I will keep a close eye on her in England so that she won't make such errors there. I'll keep an eye on you, too." She fixed Elizabeth with a steely stare and added, "As long as you and your sister follow my guidance, all will be well."

Life in England with Miss Priss sounded like prison to Elizabeth. "Miss Priscilla, Mama, Father," Elizabeth pleaded, "please believe me. I'm not proper enough to go to England. I truly did trick Annabelle into acting so rudely."

"She did, she did, she did!" ranted Annabelle.

"Elizabeth," Mrs. Cole began, "I—"

But Miss Priscilla interrupted. "You couldn't possibly be clever enough to plan such pranks, Little One!" she said condescendingly. "But oh, how you do amuse me! We'll have great fun in England. You are very funny, Elizabeth!"

❧

"No!" exclaimed Felicity when Elizabeth told her the terrible news.

43

The two friends were together at Elizabeth's house. It was just a few hours before the engagement party, and Felicity had come over to see Elizabeth in her beautiful new pink gown. "Do your parents truly want you to go to England?"

Elizabeth spoke slowly. "It seems so," she said. "They say that it will be advantageous for me and that I will be safer there."

"Oh!" exclaimed Felicity in exasperation. "Safer! 'Tis so unfair when grownups' disagreements ruin everything for their children. We did not start this fight between Loyalists and Patriots, but we have to suffer for  it. I will be miserable if you go to England, and you will be, too."

"Aye," Elizabeth agreed wholeheartedly, "especially because I will be under Miss Priss's thumb."

"Why does *she* want you to go?" asked Felicity.

"To have someone else to bully!" said Elizabeth.

"You can't go with her," said Felicity wildly. "You must run away! Or perhaps you could paint dots on yourself and pretend that you have the pox.

That would scare her! Or you could secretly practice rowing between now and the wedding, and then when you are on the ship for England, you could steal a smaller boat, jump overboard into it, and row ashore! Or you and I could both cut off all our hair and dress as boys and run off to the western wilderness together. Or we could join up with pirates, or—"

"Felicity," Elizabeth interrupted gently, "your ideas are not very practical, I'm afraid. We must think carefully. We need a good plan, and we need it quickly. We don't have much time. At the party, Miss Priscilla is going to announce that I am going to England. Once her announcement has been made in front of all my parents' friends, my parents will feel honor-bound to hold to their agreement with Miss Priscilla. So we must make Miss Priscilla change her mind about me *before* she can make the announcement. We've got to convince her that she wants to take Annabelle to England, but not *me*."

Felicity's face lit up with an idea. "You could behave very strangely at the party tonight," she said. "You could whoop and shriek and knock things over and run about madly like a crackpate."

Elizabeth giggled, but then she said, "I'm afraid that would not change Miss Priscilla's mind. She has already seen Annabelle do all of those things and more at breakfast over the last few days, and she is still taking *her* back to England."

"Oh," said Felicity. She smiled a little at the thought of what breakfast with Annabelle Bananabelle must have been like for the past few days.

Elizabeth spoke thoughtfully. "I think Miss Priscilla is pleased when we behave badly because it proves that she is right, that everyone here in the colonies is an uncivilized hot-head," Elizabeth said.

Felicity shook her head, frowning. "We are not uncivilized," she said, "and no one is a hot-head— except maybe Ben about being a Patriot. Miss Priscilla is wrong."

"She's sure she's right about that and everything else," said Elizabeth. "She enjoys fussing at Annabelle and me and telling us that we do not know the right way to act or speak or even how to dress properly, the way aristocratic ladies do in England. Of course, she thinks that the way *she* does everything is perfect and that the way *she* dresses is the height of fashion. You should see the ridiculous wig she is going to wear tonight. She brought it with her all the way from England. She is very proud about showing it off in front of all the fancy people at the party. She's very vain about it. The wig is as tall as I am! Come, I'll show you."

Elizabeth and Felicity tiptoed up the steps and into the room where the wigs were powdered. "Look," said Elizabeth. She pointed to a wig that was so tall and so heavily dusted with white powder that it looked like one of the drifts of snow outside the window. Swoops and swirls of curls wrapped around the wig and hung down from it, with bunches of flowers and ribbons and bows peeking out from among the curls.

"My!" said Felicity. "It looks so big and heavy! Her head will be awfully warm under that wig."

"Aye," joked Elizabeth. "'Tis Miss Priss who'll be a hot-head tonight!"

The two friends giggled.

Then Elizabeth looked at Felicity with a sparkle in her eyes and said, "Perhaps we should fix the wig to help Miss Priscilla keep a cool head."

"How?" asked Felicity.

Without another word, Elizabeth opened

*"Aye," laughed Felicity. "That will throw cold water on her plans!"*

the window. She scooped a handful of snow off the windowsill and packed it into a small, hard snowball. Then she very carefully wriggled her hand into the hair of the wig and hid the snowball in among the snowy white curls. Felicity caught on right away, and made a few small snowballs to hide in Miss Priscilla's wig, too. Then Elizabeth put the wig next to the open window so that it would stay very cold until Miss Priscilla put it on.

When they were finished, the two girls scampered back downstairs and collapsed against one another, weak with laughter.

"When the snowballs melt, they'll cool Miss Priscilla's head," said Elizabeth cheerfully. "I think they'll also cool her feelings toward me when she finds out that I am responsible for them."

"Aye," laughed Felicity. "That will throw cold water on her plans!"

# CHAPTER
## FOUR

# HOT-HEADS

 Elizabeth had never seen her house look as elegant as it did for the party. Light from dozens of candles made the rooms glow. The light flickered and danced on the ceilings and walls, seeming to keep time with the music the musicians were playing in the parlor. Sprigs of holly and ivy tied with red ribbons hung at the windows, and garlands of holly and ivy were looped over the doorways, on the musicians' music stands, and along the dining table. The table itself was covered with silver, crystal, and china dishes so fine that they were pearly and translucent. Even the food was beautiful! Golden pears, sweetmeats, iced cakes, nuts, and candied figs were piled high in

pyramids. In the parlor, all the furniture had been pushed against the walls to make space for dancing. The rugs had been removed and the floor had been polished until it was gleaming.

Annabelle danced past with Mr. Cole, and Elizabeth had to admit that her sister looked lovely. Annabelle's dress, made of pale yellow silk trimmed with lace, was as pretty as a snowflake. Annabelle truly was the belle of the ball. She stepped lightly, turned, curtsied, and twirled gracefully as she danced.

In fact, all but two of the dancers moved so effortlessly across the shiny floor that they seemed to be skating on smooth ice. Elizabeth watched the two awkward dancers, Miss Priscilla and Lord Harry, very closely. They made rather a mismatched couple because Lord Harry was so much taller than his sister. Elizabeth did not see how they could possibly speak to one another. Miss Priscilla was nose-to-button with Lord Harry's silver coat buttons, and Lord Harry's nose was in danger of being lost in Miss Priscilla's towering wig. Lord Harry looked too worried to speak anyway. His eyebrows were frightened high, and he doggedly steered his sister

*All but two dancers moved effortlessly across the shiny floor.*

around the dance floor as if she were an ox he was backing into the harness of a plough. Miss Priscilla was too puffed up with pride in herself and her wig to notice how gracelessly she and her partner were dancing. She had a snooty, snobbish expression on her face underneath her snowbank of hair.

Elizabeth stared at that snowbank particularly. She was worried. Surely the room was warm enough. Why weren't the snowballs melting? Oh, she wished they'd hurry! At any moment her mother might come into the parlor from the entry hall where she was greeting guests. Then Mr. Cole would stop the music and announce Annabelle and Lord Harry's engagement, and Miss Priscilla would tell everyone that Elizabeth was going to England, too. Once she did, Elizabeth would have to go.

Then, suddenly, *plink!* Elizabeth saw a droplet of water fly out from Miss Priscilla's wig and land on the floor. *Plink, plink, plink.* Three more droplets flew from the wig, sparkled as they caught the light, then plopped to the floor. More droplets hit Lord Harry's coat sleeves and left splotchy spots. The top of Miss Priscilla's wig began to look like the icing on a Christmas cake as water from the melting snowballs mixed with the white powder and made a sticky paste. Because the wig was so high, Miss Priscilla herself did not see or feel the droplets, though soon they sprayed freely from her wig as she bumpily turned and twirled, leaving a trail of tiny puddles and a trail of startled, water-spattered dancers behind her as she passed by.

When a cold, wet glob landed on Annabelle, she squealed, "Eeek!"

"What's the matter? What's the matter?" cried Mr. Cole, who was her dancing partner. He stopped dancing, and the music stopped, too.

Elizabeth held her breath as the room fell silent. All the guests turned to look at Annabelle. When they saw that she was pointing a shaky finger at Miss Priscilla's head, they all turned to stare at Miss Priscilla.

It seemed to Elizabeth that at first, Miss Priscilla did not understand what was going on. It was not until she had stood still for a moment that a water  drop slid from her wig down the center of her forehead and out to the tip of her nose. It hung there like a pearl drop, then fell to the floor with a *plop*.

Miss Priscilla looked around her feet and saw that she was encircled by drops of water that had fallen—and were still merrily dripping—from her wig.

"Oh, my!" Miss Priscilla whimpered. She clutched her wig with both hands and hurried from the room, leaving a shimmery trail of water drops behind her on the mirror-like floor.

Elizabeth spoke in a whisper that only Annabelle beside her could hear. "Gracious, Prissabelle!" she said. "Ladies in England never whimper! And surely *you* of all people must know that they never run out of the room without making a proper curtsy!"

Annabelle gasped and turned sharply toward Elizabeth. Elizabeth could tell by the look in her eyes that Annabelle knew who had made Miss Priscilla's wig melt. For a moment, Annabelle looked alarmed. Then a very odd expression crossed her face. It was just the tiniest hint of a smile.

At a signal from Mr. Cole, the music started up again and most of the dancers went back to their dancing.

Mrs. Cole hurried toward Mr. Cole and the girls, who were standing with Lord Harry.

"Miss Priscilla just rushed past me and up the stairs to her chamber," said Mrs. Cole. "Was she taken ill?"

"I believe Miss Priscilla felt a sudden chill," said Elizabeth solemnly.

Annabelle covered her mouth with her hand and made a choking sound.

"Do not be distressed, my love," Mrs. Cole said to Annabelle. "Miss Priscilla will recover, I am sure, and may return when she has fetched a wrap. Why don't you dance with Lord Harry for a while? It is getting late, and your father is about to announce your engagement to our guests. We shall have to postpone Miss Priscilla's additional good news about Elizabeth going to England, however, as Miss Priscilla most particularly wanted to announce that herself. 'Tis a pity indeed."

Elizabeth and Annabelle looked at one another eye to eye. Then, at the same time, they both said, "Indeed."

Miss Priscilla, without her wig, was waiting in the upper hallway for her brother and the Coles when they came upstairs after the last guests had departed. Elizabeth could tell from her pinched face and piercing look that Miss Priscilla was not pleased.

"Oh, my dear Miss Priscilla!" said Mrs. Cole. "I am so sorry that you left the party! You missed the announcement of Annabelle and Lord Harry's engagement. But Elizabeth explained that you felt a sudden chill. It is not a head cold coming on, I hope."

Miss Priscilla's face pinched even more. "My wig," she said in an icy tone, "was full of snow!"

"Snow?" asked Mr. and Mrs. Cole together.

"Yes," said Miss Priscilla, "and I know who put it there." She turned to Elizabeth. "You minx! You scamp! You mischievous imp! You *did* play all those tricks on your sister, and tonight you played a trick on *me!*" she said. "I've been sorely mistaken in you. I thought you'd be as easy to control as your silly sister. But now I see you for the trickster that you really are."

"I beg your pardon, Miss Priscilla!" exclaimed Mrs. Cole. She stood behind Elizabeth and Annabelle protectively. "What are you saying about my daughters?"

"What's this? What's this?!" sputtered Mr. Cole.

"Elizabeth, am I to understand that you put *snow* in Miss Priscilla's wig?"

"Yes, Father," said Elizabeth simply.

"But *why?*" asked Mr. and Mrs. Cole together.

"I had to prove to her—and to you two, as well—that I am not proper enough to go to England," said Elizabeth.

"Proper?" barked Miss Priscilla. "You're a rude, rumbustious jackanapes! I would no more take you back to England with us than I'd take a wild monkey! You are no longer invited!"

"Oh, thank you," said Elizabeth sincerely, softly, and sweetly, "for I do not wish to go."

Lord Harry surprised them all by cheering, "Right-oh, Miss Elizabeth!"

"Oh, do be quiet, Harry!" said Miss Priscilla.

"No," said Lord Harry. "This time you won't stop me, Prissy. I have something important to say. I'm going to say it and you're going to listen."

Everyone stared at Lord Harry in astonishment.

Lord Harry blushed very red, but his eyebrows were set in firm, determined straight lines. "Prissy, you usually *don't* listen to me, so I gave up trying to talk about what *I* wanted long ago," he said. "But while I've been here, I've made a friend. He's a fine fellow, and we've had good conversations about what we want to do in the future. I met him while looking at horses. His name is Ben."

"Ben?" said Annabelle, squeaking a little. "Mr. Merriman's apprentice?"

"That's the fellow," said Lord Harry. "Ben has great horse sense. He taught me that the first things to look for in a horse are bright, clear eyes and good, sound teeth."

Elizabeth chuckled. She smiled toothily and batted her eyelashes at Annabelle, who flushed.

"Ben and I agree about horses," said Lord Harry. "And even though we don't agree about the king, we do agree that a person has to fight for what he thinks is right. So Ben's joining the Patriot army as soon as he can, and I've decided to join the king's army as soon as I can."

"No!" snapped Miss Priscilla.

But Lord Harry ignored her. "Annabelle," Lord Harry said, "you are a grand girl, and very pretty, too. But I don't want to marry you. I don't want to marry anyone at all, not for a while, anyway, not until after I've been a soldier. Marrying you was all Prissy's idea and I went along because, well, because Prissy is Prissy. I am sorry. I should have spoken to you about this before your father announced our engagement, but I didn't have the courage to stand up to Prissy until I saw Miss Elizabeth do it tonight. I hope you will forgive me for breaking our engagement."

"I do, I do, I do forgive you!" exclaimed Annabelle, bouncing happily. "You are a nice young man, Lord Harry. But though I might be able to live happily with you, I could never live happily with your sister. So the truth is, I don't want to marry you, either!"

"I'm glad to hear it!" said Lord Harry, shaking Annabelle's hand heartily.

"Hmph!" Miss Priscilla snorted at Annabelle. "You know that you never would have been worthy of the respect due to the name 'Lady Lacey' anyway."

Elizabeth expected Annabelle to be crushed. But instead, Annabelle did a very surprising thing. She put her arm around Elizabeth's shoulder and said firmly, "I beg your pardon, Miss Priscilla. But what I know is that my name is just plain *Anna*belle Cole, and my sister Elizabeth has helped me see that there's nothing wrong with that—or with being who I truly am. I'd rather have people respect me for what I do than for what my name is." Annabelle grinned at Elizabeth, then said, "And I have become much too independent-minded to allow anyone to *tell* me what to do every moment of the day! I guess I had better stay here in the colonies, where people are proud of thinking for themselves."

Elizabeth grinned back at Annabelle. But she stopped grinning when she saw the grim expressions on her parents' faces.

"Elizabeth," said Mrs. Cole in a serious voice, "Miss Lacey is our honored guest. You are very wrong to have played such a childish trick on her."

"Aye," said Mr. Cole. "Apologize at once."

"Yes, sir," said Elizabeth. She turned to Miss Priscilla and said, "I beg you will forgive me, Miss Priscilla."

"Hmph!" snorted Miss Priscilla, just as angry as ever. "I wash my hands of the lot of you. Lord Harry and I will leave tomorrow at daybreak. Come along now, Harry."

Lord Harry bowed, smiled at Mr. and Mrs. Cole, and winked at Annabelle and Elizabeth. His caterpillar eyebrows had never looked so happy. Then he turned and followed Miss Priscilla, who was so angry that she had stormed off to her room without making a proper curtsy.

"Annabelle," said Elizabeth when the Laceys were gone, "are you quite sure you don't want to be Lady Lacey?"

Annabelle laughed. "I am sure," she said. "Thank you, Elizabeth, for making me realize it."

Mrs. Cole shook her head. "What am I to do with two such daughters?" she asked. "I suppose it is a good thing that you will both be near me, where I can keep an eye on you." She smiled a little and said, "Indeed, I must admit that it would have broken my heart to have you two so far away in England."

"Aye," said Mr. Cole. "Although it would have been a very good match, it is better for our family to stay together. We'll keep one another safe come what may, no matter what happens between the Loyalists and the Patriots."

❧

The Laceys left the very next morning. As soon as their carriage pulled away, Elizabeth and

Annabelle set forth for Mr. Merriman's store. Elizabeth was anxious to tell Felicity what had happened, and Annabelle *said* she wanted to look for buttons, but Elizabeth suspected that she really wanted to look for Ben. Elizabeth was so happy and excited that she flew along at a brisk clip, her feet hardly touching the bumpy brick street.

"Bitsy!" huffed Annabelle behind her. "Do slow down! Gracious! You are so bouncy!"

Elizabeth stopped short, mid-bounce. She turned to look at Annabelle and saw instantly that the friendly, grateful sister who'd spoken up to Miss Priscilla so sensibly the night before was gone, and Annabelle Bananabelle was back. Elizabeth sighed. She trudged toward Mr. Merriman's store with a heavy heart, keeping step with Annabelle.

Felicity, practically dancing with curiosity, met Elizabeth and Annabelle at the door of the store. "Do tell me!" she said. "I saw the Laceys' carriage leave this morning. What happened?"

"Well," said Annabelle grandly. "Thanks to me, all is well. Bitsy and I are going to stay here in

63

Virginia." She craned her neck to look around the store. "Is Ben here?" she asked.

"No, I am sorry, he's not," said Felicity. "He's out making a delivery."

"Harumph," grumped Annabelle. Then she flounced off to look at buttons.

When she was gone, Felicity said, "I am gladder than I can say that *you* are not going to England, Elizabeth. But I am confused. Did Annabelle say that *both* of you are staying here?"

Elizabeth nodded. "Aye," she sighed. "Annabelle is not going to marry Lord Harry. They *both* wanted to end their engagement, so there is no disgrace in it, luckily for Annabelle. You and I are stuck with Annabelle, I fear. And 'tis our own fault. We did rather too fine a job of cooling off Miss Priscilla. Now we are right back where we began with annoying Annabelle."

"Right back where we began is not such a bad place to be," said Felicity joyfully. She looked sideways at Elizabeth. "I happen to know that Ben is to make a delivery to your house later today. Shall we tell Annabelle that Ben has heard that she is not going to marry Lord Harry?"

Elizabeth caught on right away. "And so she is free to be courted!" said Elizabeth, exuberant again. "Shall we tell Annabelle that Ben is coming to call on her?"

"Oh, yes, let's!" said Felicity. "That would be very funny, Elizabeth!"

# LOOKING BACK

# COURTSHIP
# AND MARRIAGE
# IN

*A wedding portrait from the late 1700s*

Annabelle's great eagerness to marry Lord Harry seemed silly to Elizabeth and Felicity, but it would have made perfect sense to many people in England and the colonies. In the late 1700s, every girl was raised to be a wife and mother, and her future depended on making a good marriage.

A wealthy girl like Annabelle did not expect to marry for love. Instead, she hoped for a husband of wealth and social standing—someone who could preserve or improve her family's position in society. She was expected to marry a man of her own class or, even better, a man who was wealthier and more upper-class than she was.

To wealthy families, a marriage proposal was really a business proposition. Most courtships began just as Annabelle and Lord Harry's did—with letters between the families. Before the couple met, their parents exchanged detailed information about their property, wealth, and family connections, and also what the young woman would bring into the marriage as her *dowry*, or "marriage portion." This information was considered so important—and so interesting—that it was published in colonial newspapers as juicy gossip!

If both sets of parents were satisfied with the other's wealth and social position, then the courtship would begin.

Few colonial families were rich and distinguished enough to attract a marriage proposal from a noble English

*When a couple became engaged, their families might announce the news with a lavish party, like the one the Coles held for Annabelle and Lord Harry.*

family—but many would have been thrilled to! By the standards of her day, Annabelle was lucky indeed to be courted by Lord Harry Lacey.

Still, Mrs. Cole and Miss Manderly had good reasons for urging Annabelle to think carefully before agreeing to marry Lord Harry. As Lady Lacey, Annabelle would return to England and enjoy great prestige, elegant social engagements, and grand homes with many servants.

*In the 1770s, England's wealthiest and most fashionable ladies wore astonishingly huge wigs—even when visiting the colonies.*

*Most of England's noble families owned a large country house
like this one, as well as a luxurious home in or near London.*

But she would also have the heavy responsibilities of
managing these households, entertaining frequently,
and strictly following the stifling rules of polite behavior
expected of a lord's wife.

If Annabelle moved to England, she was also likely
to be separated from her parents and sister, because travel
was difficult. After Betsey Blair, a young Williamsburg
woman, moved to England following her marriage in
1769, she kept in touch with her sister Anne by letter,
but they never saw each other again.

Most serious of all, as Mrs. Cole
pointed out, once Annabelle married,
she was married forever. Divorce
was not allowed in Virginia or in

England, no matter how unhappy a marriage might be.

Still, many well-to-do girls did marry by the time they were Annabelle's age—and apparently most of them were just as eager to wed as Annabelle. In 1788, a Virginia mother wrote:

> *A Woman's happiness dependes entirely on the Husband she is united to; it is a step that requires more deliberation than girls generally take . . . at sixteen and nineteen we think everybody perfect that we take a fancy to.*

When Annabelle decided against marrying Lord Harry, she was lucky that he felt the same way. If she had backed out of the engagement without his agreement, she would have become known as a "bolter"—someone who runs away from commitments—and her hopes of making another good match would have been dim.

Nearly all women in the colonies married by their early twenties. A young woman who hadn't married by the age of 20 or 25 was considered an "old maid"!

Men and women who didn't marry had a hard time fitting into colonial society. Most colonists believed that marriage and parenthood were the natural responsibilities of *all* adults. Unmarried men were rarely elected to public office. The colony of Maryland even made bachelors pay an extra tax! A woman who didn't marry usually lived out her life in her father's or brother's house, without income, property, or children of her own.

A colonial cartoon of an unmarried woman

Women who didn't marry were often regarded with pity—or worse. A North Carolina newspaper in 1790 described unmarried women as "cranky, ill-natured, maggoty, peevish . . . good for nothing creatures."

Of course, this unflattering stereotype didn't really apply to most unmarried women. But women who deliberately *chose* not to marry and

A few women made their living at trades such as brickmaking.

who earned their own living with independence and dignity, as Miss Manderly did, were rare.

Still, such women did exist. Unlike a wife, a single woman could own property, earn wages, make contracts, and run a business. All through the colonies, there were examples of successful single businesswomen— mostly widows but some

*A Williamsburg widow, Clementina Rind,*
*published this influential newspaper.*

unmarried women, too. Some,
like Miss Manderly, taught
lessons. Several were printers, like
Clementina Rind, who published
a Virginia newspaper and was
the Colony of Virginia's official
printer in the 1770s. Other women
ran boarding houses, kept taverns, owned shops, or even
worked as carpenters, silversmiths, and shoemakers.

Despite such examples, however, most women
in the 1700s wanted their lives to revolve around
marriage and motherhood. More than likely, that
would have been not only Annabelle's ideal, but
Elizabeth's and Felicity's too—eventually!

*The warmth of*
*family life was*
*captured in this*
*portrait painted in*
*London in 1778.*

# A SNEAK PEEK AT

# MEET

*Felicity Merriman can't wait to see the new horse
at Jiggy Nye's tannery!*

elicity and Ben made their way along the dusty, wide main street of Williamsburg. It was not very busy this afternoon. The city was just begining to wake up after the hot, sleepy summer. Mrs. Vobe was welcoming some guests to her tavern. The milliner had opened the windows of her shop to catch the first fall breezes. Here and there, peeking out from behind a hedge or a fence, Felicity saw yellow flowers nodding their heads to welcome autumn.

After they delivered the oats to Mrs. Fitchett's stable, Ben said, "I can find my way to the tannery and home from here."

Felicity kept right on walking. "Mr. Nye has a new horse, and I've a curiosity to see it," she said. Felicity half expected Ben to tell her to run along home, but he didn't say anything. *Sometimes I'm glad he's so quiet,* thought Felicity. She grinned to herself.

Jiggy Nye's tannery was on the far edge of the town, out where the neat fenced yards grew ragged and pastures stretched off into the woods. Felicity could smell the tannery vats before she could see the tumbledown tannery shed. The vats were huge

kettles full of yellow-brown ooze
made of foul-smelling fish oil or
sour beer. Mr. Nye soaked animal
hides in them to make leather.

"Whoosh!" said Felicity. "The smell
of the tannery is enough to make your hair curl."

"Aye!" said Ben. "The whole business stinks."

Suddenly they heard angry shouts and a horse's
frightened whinnies.

"Down, ye hateful beast! Down, ye savage!"
they heard Mr. Nye yell.

Felicity ran to the pasture gate. She saw Mr. Nye
in the pasture, trying to back a horse between the
shafts of a work cart. The horse was rearing up and
whinnying. It jerked its head and pawed the air with
its hooves. Mr. Nye was shouting and pulling on a
rope that was tied around the horse's neck.

"I'll beat ye down, I will," yelled Mr. Nye. "I'll
beat ye!"

Ben caught up with Felicity and pulled her arm.
"Stay back," he ordered.

"No! I want to see the horse," said Felicity. She
stood behind the open gate and stared. The horse
was wild-eyed and skinny. Its coat was rough and

*"Stay back," Ben ordered.*
*"No! I want to see the horse," said Felicity.*

matted with dirt. Its mane and tail were knotted with burrs. But Felicity could see that it was a fine animal with long, strong legs and a proud, arched neck. "Oh, 'tis a beautiful horse," whispered Felicity. "Beautiful."

Mr. Nye and the horse both seemed to hear her at the same moment. The horse calmed and turned toward Felicity. That gave Mr. Nye a chance to tighten the rope around its neck. When the horse felt the rope, it went wild again. Mr. Nye was nearly pulled off the ground when it reared up on its hind legs.

"Ye beast!" Mr. Nye shouted. He glared at Ben and barked, "Help me! Get in here and grab this rope!"

Ben darted into the pen and grabbed the rope with Mr. Nye, but the horse reared and pawed the air more wildly than before.

"I'll beat the fire out of ye!" shouted Mr. Nye in a rage. He raised his whip to strike the horse.

"No!" cried Felicity. At that, the horse took off across the pasture, dragging Ben and Mr. Nye through the dust. They had to let go of the rope.

Mr. Nye waved his arms and yelled at Felicity, "Get away with ye! You've spooked my horse, ye bothersome chit of a girl."

Felicity called out, "You spooked the horse yourself. You know you did."

"Arrgh!" Mr. Nye snarled. He turned his red-rimmed eyes on Ben and growled, "What are ye doing here?"

"I've brought the bit you ordered from Master Merriman," Ben said.

Mr. Nye held out his hand. "Give it here."

Ben stepped back. "I'm to wait for payment," he said.

"Get away with ye!" shouted Mr. Nye. "Keep your blasted bit. That horse won't take the bit no matter. Go now, before I take my whip to the two of ye. Hear me?"

Ben turned to go, but Felicity backed away slowly.

She couldn't stop watching the beautiful horse. It was running back and forth across the pasture, trapped inside the fence.

"Felicity, come along!" said Ben.

Felicity turned and followed Ben, but she did not even see the road in front of her. "Isn't she beautiful, Ben?" Felicity said. "Isn't she a dream of a horse? Just once I'd love to ride a horse like that!"

"She'd be too fast for you," said Ben. "You'd never stay on her." He shook his head grimly. "Besides, that horse won't trust anyone after the way Mr. Nye is treating her. She won't let anyone on her back ever again. That horse has gone vicious."

Felicity heard what Ben said, but she didn't believe it. She'd seen the look of frantic anger in the horse's eyes. But Felicity had seen something else, too. Under the wildness there was spirit, not viciousness. Just as under the mud and burrs there was a beautiful, reddish-gold coat, as bright as a new copper penny. "Penny," whispered Felicity.

"What?" asked Ben.

"Penny," said Felicity. "That's what I'm going to call that horse. She's the color of a new copper penny. It's a good name for her, isn't it?"

"Aye," said Ben. "Because she's an independent-minded horse, that's for certain. Call her Penny for her independence, too."

Felicity smiled. From then on, she thought of the horse as Penny—beautiful, independent, bright, shining Penny. And she made up her mind to go back to the tannery to see Penny as soon as she could.

# Read All of Felicity's Stories,
available at bookstores and *americangirl.com*.

### Meet Felicity • An American Girl
Penny, the horse Felicity loves, is in trouble. Felicity must
figure out a way to help her before it's too late!

### Felicity Learns a Lesson • A School Story
Lessons about serving tea pose a problem for Felicity—
how to be loyal to her father *and* to her friend.

### Felicity's Surprise • A Christmas Story
Felicity's mother becomes terribly ill. Is Christmastide
really a time when hopes and dreams come true?

### Happy Birthday, Felicity! • A Springtime Story
Felicity overhears a message that means danger
to the colonists, and she must warn them herself.

### Felicity Saves the Day • A Summer Story
Felicity's friend Ben has run away and needs help.
Will Felicity help Ben—or tell her father where he is?

### Changes for Felicity • A Winter Story
Felicity faces many changes in her friendships
and her family as war breaks out in the colonies.

◆

### Welcome to Felicity's World • 1774
American history is lavishly illustrated
with photographs, illustrations, and
excerpts from real girls' letters and diaries.

# MORE TO DISCOVER!

While books are the heart of The American Girls Collection® they are only the beginning. The stories in the Collection come to life when you act them out with the beautiful American Girls dolls and their exquisite clothes and accessories. To request a free catalogue full of things girls love, send in this postcard, call **1-800-845-0005,** or visit our Web site at **americangirl.com**.

*Please send me an American Girl®catalogue.*

My name is _____

My address is _____

City _____ State _____ Zip _____
1961i

My birth date is _____/_____/_____ E-mail address _____
month    day    year      Fill in to receive updates and web-exclusive offers.

Parent's signature _____

*And send a catalogue to my friend.*

My friend's name is _____

Address _____

City _____ State _____ Zip _____
1225i

If the postcard has already been removed from this book
and you would like to receive an American Girl® catalogue,
please send your name and address to:

*American Girl*
*P.O. Box 620497*
*Middleton, WI 53562-0497*

You may also call our toll-free number, **1-800-845-0005,**
or visit our Web site at **americangirl.com.**

Place
Stamp
Here

PO BOX 620497
MIDDLETON WI  53562-0497